The Yard Sale

by Katherine Scraper • illustrated by B.B. Sams

Meet the Characters

Mark

Mom

Man

Boy

Boy

Girl

Mark and Mom got some tables.
Mark and Mom put the tables
in the yard.

4

5

Mark and Mom put toys
on the tables. They put clothes
on the tables. They put books
on the tables, too.

Toys

A man said, "I will get this book."
Mark said, "The book is 10 cents."
The man put a dime in the jar.

8

Books

A boy said, "Can I get this toy car?"

Mark said, "The car is 5 cents."

The boy put a nickel in the jar.

25¢

15¢

25¢

3¢

Toys

25¢

15¢

5¢

11

A girl said, "I like this doll!
I will give you 25 cents."
Mom put the quarter in the jar.

A boy said, "I have 3 pennies. What can I get?"
Mark said, "You can get 3 baseball cards."
The boy put the pennies in the jar.

25¢

15¢

Toys

15

The yard sale was over.
Mark said, "Can we
go shopping?"